THE QUEST OF THE GOLE

JOHN HOLLANDER

THE QUEST
OF
THE GOLE

DRAWINGS BY REGINALD POLLACK

ATHENEUM   NEW YORK

1966

J

3/67

For Jeremy, David and Raphael

Time erases what has been written down, just as it makes ruins of palaces. It can even destroy what has been remembered, and many of the oldest stories we know have come down to us in bits and pieces. Paper and parchment rot, clay or stone tablets break, and the memories of men invent and then believe they are remembering. The Story of the Gole is one of these old tales, and it can only be set down here at all because parts of it are still to be found in many ancient writings. We might have had the whole story in one piece, if the old tale told by a northern poet who wrote the jumpy, unrhymed lines which begin this narration had survived intact. But it did not, and many other old stories, songs, letters and histories had to be consulted. Except for the old poet of the North, none of these other singers and storytellers really knew the whole story of Strengal and Myndal and Moad and their search. That is what is told here. The three parts of it are the First Book, which introduces the story and tells of the great deeds of Strengal; the Second Book, which tells of the wanderings of Myndal; and the Third, which is of Moad. It tells as much about the Gole as is known today.

Contents

THE QUEST
OF
THE GOLE

PROLOGUE

Listen! there were lots of long
Tales that were told in times since gone:
How the brave Beowulf bought awful glory
By freeing his folk of a fearful pair,
A monster and his much more monstrous mother,
And gathering gold that a dragon guarded.
Stories that still can manage to startle us
Even though everything they are about
Hasn't been able to happen to anyone
For more years than men can ever remember:
Of Wodal, who waded through sorrowful water
In search of a sword that looked so strange
That everyone else was afraid to use it.
Or Princess Purkrasmel who prayed to her cat
In her tiny room at the top of the tower
When the dark red draperies were drawn for the night;
Of Gandil, who was given a ghastly garment

3

By the Weaving Woman, who wept when the
      weather
Was fine. Of the fire at Alfortines,
The castle on the crag that was crammed full of birds,
And how Eskal escaped with the sack of keys.
Or on the nine nights that could never have happened
How Brondala bought, for a purple bead,
From the toothless, truthless Trolls of the Road
The Flask that could only be full when empty;
How Slenga and her silly, bickering sister
Argued endlessly until they were turned
Into each other by the Apple-eater.

Long since have these stories been lost,
The tongue they were told in, forgotten today.
There is only one left. I happened to learn it
By reading the bird-writing cut in the rocks
That only the eagles visit now.
East by southeast, in the early evening,
The great, gray cliffs turn peculiarly blue.
As the solemn sun starts its last sinking,
The darkening slates on the southern summit
Can be suddenly seen to be covered with script
Like branches, or broken wings of birds.
For seven summers I tried to decipher it
In the falling, fading daylight. I failed.
And then one winter, when the bitter wind
Bit at my fingers, I found the full

4

Meaning of the marvelous marks on the rocks.
Then I translated the tale they told:
It was one of winter, a story of winds,
Of fearful freezing, but looking forward
Toward sun and the splendidness of summer
And the golden greatness of the Gole.

PART I

Way to northwest, where the water whispers
As the cold sea slips up into the saltmarshes
And frost forms at the foot of the trees,
There was a high hall. Hrimhaegl it was called,
Walled with worn stones, always wet,
Topped by tall clusters of turrets
Twinkling weakly in the wintry sun.
Tiny towns lay tumbled about
The edge of the marshes, which remained moist
For most of the year, and yellow mists
Coldly crowned over the Northern Kingdom.

It was not a particularly pleasant place.

One night in November, when the northeast wind
Hurled hailstones at the roofs of Hrimhaegl,
And an awful battering, as if of apples
Tossed from a tree, troublesomely rumbled

Above the high hall, there was heavy sorrow
Within the walls of the wet castle.
The King of the country lay quietly dying.
In the high-beamed hall there was no harping
Nor telling of tales, and a terrible hush
Hung even over the hunting-dogs
Who lay like slates on the long floor.
In all the corners of the cold kingdom
There was sorrowful silence, except for the noise
Of the harshly howling wind, and the hail.
The King had been careful and kind, and his wisdom
Renowned throughout the North, but now
His wife was weeping and wailing in a corner,
Looking unlike a queen. The Lords
Of the Marshlands met and muttered together
Outside the open door of the empty
Throneroom. Throughout the hall, only three
People were not either praying or planning:
Each of the princes was all alone
In his own royal room; all remembered
Their father's final words, that a few
Minutes before, they had heard him murmur
In the dying light of his life and the day.

"My sons," he said, with a sad face,
"I feel the finishing of my life, and before
I die, one duty remains to be done.
A king's crown is heavy. This country

8

Is cold and wild. I wish that I could
Simply say that my eldest son,
Strengal the Strong, with the tightest-strung
Bow in all my boroughs will be
Made King; and that you, clever Myndal,
And you, dear Moad, will remain dutiful,
Being good brothers and brave advisers,
Helping to rule from Hrimhaegl.
But alas, dear boys, this cannot be!
Our kingdom is under a cruel curse.
I did something dreadful one day long ago,
And one of the Pale, Unhappy People
Who live in the loam by the Lost Ponds
Punished me, putting a powerful spell
Over me, all of my days. Their awful
Magic made my life miserable.
I was forced to forget that most unfortunate
Deed that I'd done, and since that day
No wisdom can tell me what it was,
No other magic can help me remember."

"Did you steal something?" Strengal asked.
"Did you murder someone?" demanded Myndal.
"Did you make evil magic?" muttered Moad.

"I'll never know. And even now,"
The King continued, "that I am close
To dying, my doom's meaning is denied me,

9

It is ghastly to go through life with a grim
Curse whose cause is kept secret
Even from him on whose head it fell.
For seventeen years I have seldom slept,
I've known all night that I should never
Be cured of this care, and only with the cries
Of soaring sea-birds, when the stars are pale
Toward morning, does my mind mercifully rest.
But there is more to my misery even
Than this, for whoever inherits all
My kingdom and carries my carved crown
Upon his head, will also have heaped
That spiteful spell upon his spirit.
Strengal and Myndal and Moad, I must
Protect you from a punishment
Meant for me. Thus none of you may
Become the King after I am cold
And in my grave in the gray ground."

"Who will be strong and govern?" asked Strengal.
"Who," asked Myndal, "will be mild and merciful?"
"Who will mind all that matters?" cried Moad.

"The country will be cold," said the King, their father,
"And will suffer sorely even in summer.
You must cure the kingdom of its curse,
And lighten the land of its load of woe.
It will be no easy, tedious task

10

Like hewing wood or hauling water:
I can't tell you how to accomplish the cure.
But it must be made. Now, send for your mother;
Bless you, dear boys; be brave when I'm dead;
Have good hope, and you will inherit
All the long lands that lie in the North."
And so saying, the sad old King
Had finally died, just an hour before.

Moad and Myndal were meditating
In their chilly chambers: the heavy charge
Placed upon them, and their last promise
To their father before he left for the far-off
Lands beyond Living, made them lonely,
Somehow. Strengal, the oldest, was staring
Angrily out through the open window
That looked toward the Land of the Lost Ponds,

Angry at all the evil power
Of the curse of the Pale, Unhappy People.
Strengal struck the stone casement
And a spider spinning a wasp-attracting
Trap tumbled from his trembling web.

"How can I help, here at Hrimhaegl,"
Pondered the prince, "to rid my people
Of all this anguish? I must go away
And seek out the source of the evil spell,
Find out what, in fact, my father did
And how we might get him to be forgiven."

But no answer came from the cold stones
Nor any response from the spider, who sped
Across to a dark and dusty corner.

Strengal stood with a stern look,
Gazing across the grim glades
That hung below the hill of Hrimhaegl,
Hour after hour, while all about him
His family prepared for his father's funeral.
Nor did he emerge from his own unhappy
Room till the royal guard was ready
For the mournful march, and the household musicians
Had all assembled outside the hall.
Myndal and Moad and their mother, weeping,
Fell into single file, and the flaring

Funeral fire was lit with flints
Chopped from the roof of the royal chamber.
Then he appeared, the oldest prince,
Strengal, strumming an unstrung harp,
Making a mournful music of silences,
Gazing down at the gray ground.

As the long line of loving mourners
Moved toward the mound where mighty flames
Roared, ready to receive in fire
The corpse of the kindest of northern kings.
Only Strengal stood still,
Hearing the harpers, his head lowered,
All alone till the funeral was over.
And afterwards, that evening, he ate
Next to nothing, and in the night
He walked along the wide walls
Of Hrimhaegl, heavy walls that hung
Sloping, slantward to the sea that slopped
At the base of its bastions, on the bare cliffs,
As if to avoid the awful emptiness
Of the wide ocean. Awake, and seeing
The boundless black of the sea before him,
Strengal strode, till striking clocks
All over the castle announced the approach
Of the dark dawn of the next day.
Then Strengal stretched out on some straw
That lay on the walk of the western wall

And slept sadly, having decided
What he would do when he had awakened.

The next morning was mild. Myndal
Slept soundly, and so did Moad,
Awakening after eleven. But Strengal
Was up early. He eagerly ran
Through the cold corridors of the castle.
He had the hardiest horse saddled,
Provisions prepared and packed for a journey,
His sword sharpened, its scabbard shined,
And his armor made ready. He ran to his mother's
Chamber, and stood on the chilly steps
That led to the long window overlooking
The saltmarshes. The morning sun
Crept slowly across the cracks of the stones
On the floor as he faced his mother, then fell
At her feet, to bid her his farewell.
The old Queen wept; then, quickly wiping
Her tears away, she told him to take
Heed for his health on his hard journey.

"Where in the world will you wander," she asked.
"What will you seek on the wild seas
Or under the sweep of the wide sky?"

"Somewhere outside the slanting walls
Of Hrimhaegl there has to be

14

An answer to all the awful questions
That seethe inside my head," he said.
And straightaway Strengal instructed
His mother, mentioning the miseries
Of the curse. "I must keep my vow to discover
The source of all our sorrow. I'll seek
The people who live by the Lost Ponds
And force them, with fierce strength, to confess
What the deed was that Father did,
And somehow, I'll make amends." He smote
His sword against the stones of the floor.

His mother was silent, then said, "My son,
When you and your brothers were young boys
One midsummer night a new nursemaid
Who came from across the eastern country
Fell ill. She lay for hours and hours,
Tossing and turning and tearing her hair,
As if something horrible hid in her head,
Then settled into a sound sleep.
But before she fell into silence, she fixed
Her eyes on an easterly window, and, over
And over, announced in an anguished voice:
'STRENGAL WILL STRIKE OUT OVER THE MOUNTAIN,
MYNDAL WILL MOVE AROUND THE MOUNTAIN,
MOAD WILL BE BORNE BEYOND THE MOUNTAIN.'
What could that mad nursemaid have meant?
We never knew; and only now

That you're setting out on such a search
Do the poor girl's words appear important."

"What became of her when she awoke?"
Strengal asked. "Strange to say,"
The Queen continued, "she quit her sickness
Suddenly, when the sun was setting,
Left Hrimhaegl, and headed for her home
Far away in the Eastern Islands."

"Do you know her name?" "No," said the Queen,
"But Wyrdwita was what the other
Girls in the castle came to call her."

"Well, that's all one to me. You must wake
Myndal and Moad, as soon as I've mounted
My horse, and let them hear what I've heard,"
Said Strengal. He stretched, and strapped his sword
Against his armored side. "I'm off!"
He said, "The sun is slanting up
Toward noon." Then he turned and gently touched
His mother's hand and made hurriedly
For the door, dashing down steps
And out to the old eastern courtyard.
He hauled his horse's reins around,
Took a last look at the tall towers
Of Hrimhaegl, hanging above him,
And galloped out of the eastern gate,

16

Spurring his horse. "What starts out slowly
May end in a minute," an old man muttered
Who lowered the latticed gate as he left.
"What starts in a minute," mused Strengal's mother
In her chilly chamber "may chance to last
As long . . . as long as a lifetime." She looked
Out of her window, over the wild
Marshy fields at the moving figure
Of Strengal, straining his hurrying horse.

Many a mile over ice and mud
He rode, until it was time to rest
His horse on the hard gray ground
Beside the road. Then, ready to ride
On again, Strengal's eye
Was struck by something rather strange
Tied to the trunk of a nearby tree.

It looked like a letter with a large, red
Seal, but as Strengal stole closer
He blinked, for he saw a bound book
Covered with writing he couldn't read
With a crimson blot of blood at the bottom
Of one of its open pages. He plucked
At the knot that tied it tight to the tree,
But was unable to open it; only
A slim strand of golden silk
Held it there, but hard as he tried
It would not be undone. Then, all of a sudden

    This part of the telling of the story of the Gole breaks
off here. The tale of the northern poet who transcribed
the strange bird-writing on the rocks was partially
lost. We would never know the full story of what
happened to Strengal, or to Myndal and Moad, were it
not for the fact that other writers in prose and poetry
seem to have known it also.

    We must depend on them for much of the rest of it.
They wrote in various languages; they must have
heard parts of the story in strange ways, and sometimes
names get slightly changed. For example, we know
from many of the Tellers of Tales that Strengal must
have come upon the Bleeding Book of Ballydon,
which had been stolen from the Eastern Islands some
years before by pirates. They sailed their flat, round
ships across the ocean, divided up their treasure, and

fell to fighting among themselves. Only one of them remained alive. He took the treasure and escaped, but before he left, he happened to open the beautiful leather and gold-bound book to a page that had been blank before. Imagine his surprise when he read the following written in it:

THEY SAILED THEIR FLAT, ROUND SHIPS ACROSS THE OCEAN, DIVIDED UP THEIR TREASURE, AND FELL TO FIGHTING AMONG THEMSELVES. ONLY ONE OF THEM REMAINED ALIVE. HE TOOK THE TREASURE AND ESCAPED, BUT BEFORE HE LEFT, HE HAPPENED TO OPEN THE BEAUTIFUL LEATHER AND GOLD-BOUND BOOK—

The pirate was too terrified to turn the page, not wanting to read about what he was doing while he did it, and certainly not wanting to find out what he would be doing next. In great fear of the magic of the book, he tied it to a tree with a golden cord from his treasure-trove, packed what he could upon his back, buried the rest, and fled across the cold, marshy fields.

Ever since then, the book had hung on the tree, bleeding from a small wound at the bottom of one page. Everyone who saw it could read about how he had just come upon it, and, if he wished, could read about what was going to happen to him next. Few cared to do this.

Now we know that Strengal had come upon the Bleeding Book. Curiously enough, it is from the author of *The Rime of Rudolph* that we learn it. Writing in his own language, he tells us of how his own hero consulted the Bleeding Book after making a hard journey to find it. Then he gives us a short history of the book itself, and at one point he mentions how

> The oldest son of Castle Rimell
> Saw the book and read it well,
> Read of how he traveled far
> His strong back turned to the Northern Star,
> Searching for the famous Gole
> Over the seas that toss and roll,
> Finally finding wealth and glory,
> But this is part of another story . . .

"Castle Rimell" is Hrimhaegl as it would have come to be pronounced in another language and its oldest son would, of course, be Strengal.

We may guess that Strengal read in the book about his own search for the Gole. He would have been most puzzled, for he did not know what it was, nor what it had to do with his real quest, which was for the nature of his father's offense, and for the means of taking the curse away from himself, his brothers and the kingdom.

Still greatly puzzled, then, he left the book below the tree trunk on which he had found it, spurred his horse, and headed on toward the land of the Lost Ponds. He rode for three days and nights, stopping only to sleep and to eat some of the food he had brought with him. As he rode, the air grew colder, but less damp, and the countryside became less marshy and more hilly, covered with huge rocks and boulders. What trees there were grew twisted and short. All was silence, for there were no birds. Strengal stopped for a while, and when the panting of his horse and the beating of his own heart had quieted, he thought, for a moment, he could hear the sound of the sea. But then there was nothing; what he had taken for sound was only re-membering. He was far from home.

Strengal looked about him. By now, he should have reached the Lost Ponds, wide shallow lakes hidden behind small hills. Perhaps he had lost his way. Then, looking down the narrow path ahead of him he saw a short, gnarled old man struggling under a heavy load of twigs and kindling wood. As he approached, Strengal called out to him.

"Am I on the way to the Lost Ponds, old man?"

"Yes and no," replied the other, dropping his load of wood with a sigh.

"Do you always answer in riddles?" Strengal asked.

"Only when the questions make me," said the old man. "You're right on the way to where they were. But if you keep going that way, you won't find them. They dried up three years ago, and the Pale People who had lived near them all went away."

21

"Where did they go?" asked Strengal.

"Far away, to the South, to look for new lakes, I suppose. They will wander far," the old man added, "and by the time their travels are ended, they will have become a different people."

"That doesn't help me at all," said Strengal. "I needed to find out from them the answer to a terribly important question. Now I may never even be able to find *them*."

"Well," said the old man, "I'm sure I can't be of any help. I'd like to do you a favor, but if you have terribly important things on your mind, helping you might get me entangled in all sorts of messes and troubles. Which I don't need," he continued, picking up his bundle of wood, and heading slowly down the road again. "But as the Pale People used to say, 'the hardest answer to the hardest question lies in the Gole.' I'm sure I don't know what that means, but it sounds like good advice. Good-bye," and the old man's last words trailed behind him over the dusty road.

Strengal was more perplexed than ever. This was the second time on his journey that he had heard of the Gole; he knew no more about what it was than he did the first time. As he struck out southward, across the cold hills and through occasional patches of scrubby forest, still hoping to pick up the trail of the Lost Ponds people, he wondered more and more about this. For three wearying months, Strengal rode resolutely toward warmer countries. He conducted himself as a prince should, and we know from many different stories about his adventures on the way. He helped one village to capture the dreadful Flaming Deer that ran through its street each night, setting fire to the thatched roofs of the houses. The Ballad of the Deer, first written down hundreds of years later, still preserves part of the story:

> It burned across the fields that night
> *Hey, ho, the Flaming Deer!*
> And set the haystacks all alight,
> But now its fire is quenchèd quite.
> *Hushaby-low and never fear.*
>
> And now he comes into the town
> *Hey-ho, the Flaming Deer!*
> Where the strong soldier pulls him down
> And wraps him up gaily in his gown.
> *Hushaby-low and never fear.*
>
> The bright deer's fire is failing fast
> *Hey, ho, the Flaming Deer!*
> And now the sparks have died at last
> And all his terror is long since past.
> *Hushaby-low and never fear!*

We also know that it was Strengal who rescued the

Queen of the Lakes from a strange band of robbers who roamed the vast plains and lived in large, egg-shaped tents. Some weeks after that, and some distance to the south, he caught the Monstrous Pike in the moat of Castle Cauchemord that was deadlier than a crocodile. As the old story goes, "Then did a young warrior ride down from the North, with his name and his fame flying before him. And the Lord of Cauchemord was fain to leave the Castle because of the murderousness of the Great Pike, but the young warrior Strengel did ask of him 'My lord, what do you have that is most of value in all your house?' The Lord did answer him 'My silver net, worked in the East with as much craft as if there had been magic in it.' And 'My Lord,' said Strengel, 'will you venture this net for to obtain the safety of your castle?' 'That I will do,' said my Lord of Cauchemord. And he would fain have thrown his net into the moat, but Strengel restrained him by saying, 'No, my Lord, I, too, must venture something' and he did grasp the net and leap into the green moat and did vanish beneath the lily-pads. And my Lord of Cauchemord would weep and mourn for the loss of his net and of his champion, but soon the waters parted and Strengel did swim up to the surface with a tiny silver fish, and it was wrapped in a net of rope. 'Here is your enemy,' he said, 'and here is your net, and there has been some magic hereabouts, but that is all one with me.' And my Lord did feast him and send him on his

24

way with great rejoicing."

But through all of these adventures, Strengal never forgot his mission. As he kept moving southward, it was strange, too, even stranger than some of his adventures, that wherever he went, he would hear some mention of the Gole. People told him puzzling things, such as that the answers to all questions lay in it, or that it was something one had to look for, or that it was very well hidden and even more valuable; but nobody seemed to know exactly what it was. Strengal began to realize that it must be part of some priceless treasure, and as his quest for the Pond people began to prove more and more fruitless, he thought from time to time of striking out after the Gole itself. Perhaps this would help him in his terrible difficulty.

He had already begun to dream of finding the Gole. Sometimes as he lay in a comfortable chamber in some large castle whose Lord was his host for the night, or as he made a soldier's bed of some dried rushes under the stars, he would see in his sleep some shining, golden cup or bowl, protected by fierce warriors or perhaps by some flame-breathing monster. Just after he had finished a battle with these guardians, Strengal's dream would end.

After months of wandering, Strengal reached the Southern Sea. We know from the Court Historians of the Empress of the East that a brave and resourceful man from far away to the northwest served as captain in her special legion of guards, a man whose name is spelled Strengollos in the court records. Strengal must have served the Empress for over a year; there are records of his fighting valiantly on the eastern borders, and of being recalled to the Empress' Great City in triumph. But then all mention of him ceases. We hear of Strengal again in the *Tale of Tobol*, and of how a brave young warrior, wandering far from home in search of a magical cup (for the Gole is not mentioned in the *Tale of Tobol*) led a group of prisoners in a great escape from the King of the Ruined City. And even here we read of how Strengal would stay awake at night, during the famous month-long march across the desert to the sea, thinking by himself as he stood looking to the north. As the *Tale of Tobol* puts it:

And while the others took their nightly rest
The brave Strengallo always kept himself
Apart, high on a sand-hill, with his head
Turned not to the mountains to the West,
Nor to the ruined walls whence they had fled
Far to the South, across the sand so red,
Nor to the Eastern Desert's level shelf,
But North, North to the sea! as if he felt
That only from the North could come his strength.

When he had reached the sea, Strengal did not sail off on a boat with the other captive princes. In the sea-port town to which he had led them, he heard tell of

26

a great golden cup which lay hidden on the other side
of a huge mountain to the west. With some of the gold
he had earned in the service of the Empress and as gifts
from the many grateful people he had helped in his
travels, he outfitted a caravan and set out for the
mountain.

We shall have to guess, for the old stories do not say,
how much Strengal longed for his home country, for
his mother and Myndal and Moad. He had been away
from home for almost three years, and he was no
closer to learning the secret of his father's guilt than he
had been when he started. He had thought of the Gole
constantly, through all his hardships and glories. There
was no doubt in his mind that the cup that lay before
him on this wearying journey meant the end of his
wandering.

After many days and nights of marching, a great
mountain loomed into view on the horizon. It was a
very long one, stretching to the left and right as far as
the eye could see, blending into a range of hills on
either side. The setting rays of the sun struck at its
snow-covered summit, and were reflected back onto
neighboring peaks, bathing them in red. As Strengal
approached the mountain with his men, he remembered what his mother had told him of the words of
the poor nursemaid Wyrdwita when he was a boy:
"Strengal will strike out over the mountain." He knew
now that this prophecy was to be fulfilled, and without

giving any other plan a thought, he led his men with their mules and camels to the base of the mountain, built a camp there, and set off the next morning with a trusty few. They began boldly to climb up the great peak.

They climbed until they were exhausted, and then Strengal led them on to climb some more. A day passed, and they were still only halfway up. But Strengal seemed to be driven by something stronger than weariness, and by the morning of the third day, he had reached the summit.

Stretched out before him lay the most beautiful valley Strengal had ever seen. The morning sun was coming up behind a deep bowl-like lake, ringed with small hills; the valley itself encircled this lake, curving up to meet the mountain, and flowing out as far as the eye could see. A gentle river led from the lake off into the distance, and the green of fields and forests looked even more brilliant than the gold of the shining water of the lake. Strengal and his men descended the mountain by an easy path which lay before them.

But all was not completely well with this beautiful place. As they reached the bottom of the path early that afternoon, a sudden darkness fell about them, as if a black cloud had flown quickly from afar across the face of the sun. It proved to be a huge bird, taller than a camel when standing, as wide as the smaller courtyard at Hrimhaegl when aloft. Its wings made a rush-

28

ing noise like the roar of waterfalls.

"Let us leave this place," exclaimed the bravest of Strengal's men, a soldier named Agaric. "There is no treasure and no cup. That monstrous bird is the only thing that has ever frightened me."

"No," replied Strengal. "That lake looks like a bowl of gold, and I am sure that it is what I have been looking for." But Agaric lowered his eyes to the ground as the great dark bird settled to the ground, square in the middle of a road leading to the lake from where they stood.

"I have fought many battles," Agaric continued, holding his hands over his eyes. "But I know that now is the time not to fight. We will go back over the mountain."

"And I shall not," said Strengal. "You may go if you choose."

"That we will," said the others. "You are a fool to stay. If this place were not really nasty, people should have built a great city here centuries ago. Look, there is no one. Stay, then, and have the bird for company." Agaric looked sadly at Strengal as the others turned back up the mountain path. "I would stay with you," he said, "because you seem to be a hero as well as a prince. But somehow, I know that I must not stay. And somehow I know that you must not, either."

But Strengal was already advancing down the road, his eyes fixed only upon the beautiful lake. Agaric

29

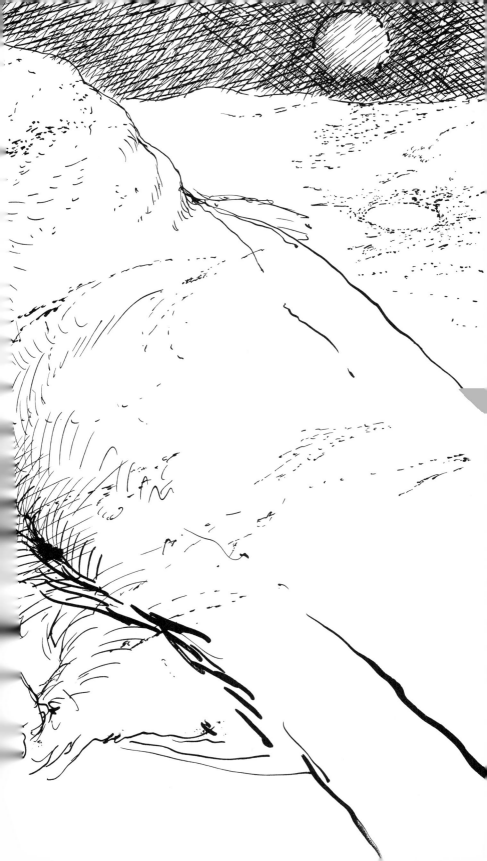

stood for a while, watching him move across the valley, which was now painted a violent red by the sunset. He watched until Strengal seemed no more than a speck; then he turned and followed the other men back across the mountain.

As Strengal drew nearer to the dreadful bird, the sun began to disappear in the west, the wind blew coldly down from the mountain, and the red color of the landscape turned slowly to a dark purplish-gray. The bird seemed to be awaiting him. It gazed down the road with huge, milky-white eyes that had no pupils at all, as big around as small saucers. It spread its huge wings like a pair of horrible black tents, parted its gray beak and flexed a pair of talons whose claws were as big as short swords. But Strengal moved on fearlessly, thinking only of the golden lake and how he must reach it. The wind blew higher as he unbuckled his sword, and finally, with a rush even stronger and louder than the wind, the bird flapped its wings and rose up to its full height. Strengal gave a sigh of sorrow and a shudder of cold and fear, and ran toward the bird, trying to get past its horrible beak.

Of Strengal's fight with the bird, we know only that it lasted all night, under the moon that repainted the valley with silver. A huge black shadow and another tiny one were engaged in a slow combat and all their struggling was a shadow too. Only toward morning did the battle speed up, and as the sun broke over the

32

valley, Strengal finally triumphed by rushing beneath the bird's throat, missing the slash of its talon, and plunging his sword into the monster's throat. The creature tumbled about him, and a stream of thick, dark blood flowed from the wound, seeping into the ground and hardening quickly into a kind of red clay. Strengal fell to the ground himself, exhausted, but after a few minutes of rest rose to his feet again and ran, staggering with weariness to the edge of the cup-shaped lake.

He knew that, at last, he was at the end of his journey. The sky was very clear and blue above him. Still panting with thirst and weariness, he fell to his knees at the edge of the shining water, and with a cry of joy lowered his hands into its clear depth, raised them to his mouth, and drank.

And suddenly, the air was full of the songs of many birds that he had not heard before. He looked about him, and the beauty of the valley now seemed overwhelming. "I must never leave this wonderful place," he murmured to himself. "I shall go back over the mountain only to bring others here, to farm the land and fish the river and build a great city. Here is beauty and peace and fair weather, and the only evil thing hereabouts is dead. I shall be the King of the City, King . . . King . . ."

But he had forgotten his name!

And with the memory of who he was vanished all

recollection of Hrimhaegl, his mother and brothers, and the task he had set himself. Even the mysterious Gole itself was gone from his thoughts. But somehow, the beauty of the valley made this not at all frightening. The magic of the waters of the lake was a good and soothing one. Anyone who drank it forgot his cares and troubles along with his name. But Strengal would never find the Gole, nor solve the puzzle of the curse upon his father. It was almost as if, good and brave as he was, he had failed, somehow, to pass a kind of test. But all he could feel was the joy of peace and discovery of something beautiful. Only for a moment did he realize that he did not know who he was. "Well, never mind," thought Strengal, "this is a new place for the lives of men and it should have a new man as king." And back he went, over the mountain to the nearest city. There he found many people, tired of war and bad kings and famine and storms at sea, and they followed him back, with many animals and wagons, to the beautiful valley and the golden lake. And there indeed they built up a great city, and there Strengal ruled as king for many years. He took the name of Anomos the First, and married a wife and she bore sons to succeed him. The little city and all its inhabitants prospered in peace, and the sun always shone on the valley.

And far, far away to the northwest, the cold castle called Hrimhaegl stood in a damp, marshy kingdom.

34

The rain and the hail and stormy waves of the sea beat about its slanting walls, and the sun, when it appeared at all, shone weakly in the gray sky.

PART II

Now, while all this was happening, Myndal and Moad must have been alone with their mother in Hrimhaegl. None of the old stories tells us exactly how long they waited for news of Strengal, nor when it was that Myndal went to his mother and told her that he, too, must leave home. It is strange that, while Myndal would soon find himself in search of the Gole, he did not know it then.

The story of their farewell was told by the poet of the North who started our tale, but this part of his poem was lost in the fire at the library of Sfarim Dor, far to the southeast. It is not hard to imagine what happened, though. After weeks of waiting in a cold season, after months of beginning to forget in the thin summer sunlight, Myndal awoke one morning and walked out on the battlements. Staring eastward, he may have seen a great bird drifting across the yellowing sky. Or he may merely have watched wing-like ripples in the water of a puddle blown by the morning wind. Perhaps he took up his harp and sang one of the old watch-songs:

> Bird from the North
> As white as snow,
> Winging from where
> I'll never go!
>
> Bird from the South,
> As green as leaves,
> Somewhere in summer
> The forest grieves!
>
> Bird from the West
> As gray as rain,
> Hovering over
> The storming main!
>
> Bird from the East
> As dark as a swallow,
> Seeing your swiftness,
> I must follow.

The last sounds of the song still sighing like a wind through the strings of his harp, Myndal would then have walked slowly into his chamber, imagining his brother's back as he rode away eastward. And he must have gone to his mother and said, "I must go after Strengal."

"Why?" she would have asked.

"Because I saw a bird this morning."

"Not because you want to find him? Or help lift the curse on our land?"

"I have wanted to do these things for months, and am still here. But today I shall go."

"Because you saw a bird?" She would have sighed and shaken her head.

"Yes, Mother."

And without really knowing why, or where, or how he was going, Myndal set forth that evening. Unlike Strengal, he chose not to ride but to travel by water, along a river that flowed from the east into the sea. He left Hrimhaegl, carrying his harp and walking down to the edge of the river.

The palace boatman led Myndal to a place of flat rocks where several boats lay overturned to dry. "Which one will you have, Prince Myndal?" he asked.

Myndal inspected the boats. There were long, pointed skiffs of the northern lake-riders and broad, flat rafts, covered with cowhides, for use across the marshes. And there was one of the western round-boats, that lay like a dish in the water and sailed in circles unless carefully guided. Myndal chose one of these, thinking "A long boat is swiftest, a raft is safest, but a round boat may take me anywhere." And he climbed into it, set sail, and moved off upstream.

We do not have to guess about the next part of

Myndal's journey, for another fragment from the
northern poet's tale survives. It tells us how the setting
sun

made red the river,

Gaily gilding the boat's gunwale and
Painting in pink its proud sail.
Myndal moved through the murmuring water,
Then darkness began to drop through the air
And, wearied of steering and watching the water,
He roped his boat to a broken rock
Among some reeds, and made ready
To rest for the night. When he arose
The bright morning sun blinded
His eyes for a bit, but on the bank
A stout man stood and stared at him.

In a minute Myndal could make him out
Among the many reeds by the river.
The broad man whispered, bending down,
"It's a grim going, against the current."

"It's worse than that," Myndal muttered.

"Why are you fighting the water's will?"

"Searching for Strengal, my strong brother
Who left us to look for the Pale People,"
Said Myndal, "many months ago."

"They're gone for good. About your brother
I know nothing at all. What now?
Where will you look for what is lost
Far beyond finding forever?"

"Are you setting me riddles, stout one?"
Asked then Myndal, angrily.

"No. But I know enough of them:
What's at the end of everything?"

"*The last of it is the letter 'G.'*
Good-bye. I am going." And Myndal began
To unwrap the rope from the piece of rock.

"You're right as a road," replied the fat man
After a moment or two of musing,
"But the answer that I was always told
Was *The Great Gole*. Where are you going?"

"On to the East," answered Myndal,
Looking away with lowered eyes.
"But what in the world is the Great Gole?"

"I don't know definitely what,
But people speak of it. Possibly
A something lost so long ago
That only its name now remains known.
Why do you gaze at the gray water?"

"To look below your words and learn
What's buried beneath. Ah well, good-bye;
A name by itself is nothing at all,"
Myndal remarked, as his massive sail
Billowed wildly in the bright wind,
And straight upstream he sailed once more.

Ever on to the East he went,
Napping each night beneath his sail
The while the wide waters of the river
Rumbled, and rocked his round-boat.
Sometimes he spoke to sailing people
On large rafts, lying flat
In the rolling river; sometimes he rowed,
Straining against the stream's gushing
Whenever the wind unwound to a whisper.
But always on toward the eastern lands
He kept his course, and carefully
Guided his gliding, circular boat.

Nowhere, and never was there news of Strengal
Or the people who lived by the Lost Ponds.
Myndal moved among the towns
Lying along the low banks
Of the rushing river. He rowed and sailed
From place to place, and people everywhere
Shook their heads and showed no sign
Of helpfulness. And here and there

41

Mention was made to Myndal of great
Treasures and tasks that too many men
Had failed to find or to fulfill.

And sometimes secret things were said
In whispers around the wavering flames
Of firelight on frosty evenings
As fall followed the fullness of summer
About the boundless beauty of something
Called the Gole. Recounting what they
Had really only read of in books
Or heard of in the hush of half-darkness,
On other evenings, elsewhere, they told
Myndal of how mysterious
A thing it was. He thought of what
It could possibly be: perhaps a cup,
A gleaming, golden Gole, guarded
In a dark den by a dragon somewhere,
Or else some object utterly magical,
Changing its form when it chanced to be seen
Or maybe making a stronger magic
More like a living thing, some kind
Of growing Gole, that gleamed and dimmed
As a caterpillar can become
A shimmering moth, but keeping its shape
For ages and ages, only changing
When men had managed almost to forget
What it had, actually, ever been.

Myndal mused on all these matters
As the days became colder and shorter
Until one night he neared a place
Where great open pastures appeared
To have sunk silently into soft rock
Right by the river: he had reached, he knew
The place where some ponds had disappeared
By drying up. His drifting boat
Moved inshore, and Myndal was sure
That the Pale People had left this place.

Sadly Myndal unslung his harp
And sang to himself as the slopping water
Brushed his boat against the gray
And ragged rocks by the river's edge.

And here the northern poet's story breaks off again,
and even the part of the page with Myndal's song on
it has been torn away. Perhaps that is best, for what he
sang may have been too sad even to imagine. Some
records remain of the next part of his journey, though,
and we know that he must have proceeded onward by
boat and tied up at the tiny harbor of the river-city of
Ravenda which is only a few days' sail from the place
where the Lost Ponds used to be. He must have been
mournful about his search, for Strengal was as lost to
him as the water of the Lost Ponds.

The *Red Book of Ravenda*, in which the Duke's scribe

kept the records of what occurred in the city, tells of Myndal's arrival there. It says "and in that month" — and this must have been November — "there did come from the western part of the river the Clever Man in the strange round boat that twisted about in the river water. He was tall and did stare at the ground even when he talked. And he did make his home here in our city, learning our language, and living in a cave by the bay. In the city square by day he sang songs, and in his cave by night he untwisted riddles. He could sing songs of the North and of the West, and his cleverness was great. Fromu, the wise-man, asked him where time will end: 'Where it began' he did answer. The Duke asked him how a good man rules a city: 'The way he rules himself' he replied. And he did ask our oldest and wisest men, in return, about a prince named Strengal, and they could tell him nothing. And sometimes he would ask about something called a Gole of which we had never heard. One spring day, when the river-birds returned from the South, he said that he would leave our city, and there was no rejoicing at his going. He left in his round-boat, sailing upstream toward where the river becomes a rushing brook and where our boats have never gone."

Myndal moved onward that spring, stopping at villages along the stream, carefully handling his boat among the rocks as the river narrowed. He became well known as a singer of tales and songs among these eastern villages and for years afterward people would speak of the young man who stayed with them only for a night or two, staring at the ground when he talked or listened, and raising his eyes only when he sang. These people never forgot Myndal, and some of the old sayings of the East seem to refer to him—things like "As wise as a Western Singer" or "He who tells strange tales at night will leave before the morning light" are still said to this day.

By the early summer, Myndal had reached a fork in the Eastern River, and had turned back along the stream that flows north again. One of his songs has come down to us in the famous *Northeast Songbook*, and although some people think that its title, "Myndl-Song," means a kind of magic, we can be very sure that it was one of those that Myndal was making up for himself as he journeyed on and on, with little hope of finding his brother or untwisting the riddle of his father's curse. The song goes like this:

> My oars, like long arms, stir
> The rimed and chilly sea
> And icy-feathered birds
> Call out, but not to me.
>
> My sail, empty of wind,
> Lies like a ruined tent;
> The last light breeze has gone,
> Whimpering as it went.

45

My dreams spin round at night
As does my boat by day;
How will I ever find out
If I have lost my way?

By the time that Myndal had got to making songs
like this one, we can be sure that he felt almost hopeless
about his search. At every place that he stopped, he
asked more and more questions, more and more sadly.

But it seems that he gave up enquiring about Strengal
after a while, and about his father's misdeed after not
much longer. Instead, he always kept asking about the
Gole. He was told many different tales, few of which
he believed, but about all of which he wondered.
Always he grew more and more famous as a singer of

songs and a teller of tales. An old book of stories credits him with having first told the story of Sansombar's Search for his Own Shadow. Another writer says, at the beginning of the *Tale of the Missing Month of May*: "I heard this first from Myndal of the Wide Mind, one wild night when the high fires [the writer must have meant the northern lights] were sinking above the hills and spilling pink on the black shadows."

All of Myndal's tales, if he did invent every one of those ascribed to him, seem to have been about quests and searchings. While some of them were like the fine old stories of battles with dragons and journeys in ships of a hundred heroes, others were strange and sad and puzzling to the people who heard them. As time went on, Myndal's own journey became as puzzling to his audiences as some of these tales were. "Why leave us?" they would ask as, one fine morning, the fluttering of a gull might draw his attention to his boat and to departing. Myndal would seldom answer, but would stare at the ground and smile as he took his farewells. He was offered gold and jewels in many places, but everywhere he only took what he needed for the next few days.

Myndal wandered as far as Strengal had, and as long. Everywhere he went, he asked of the Gole and learned new songs and ways of making them up. From a singer of the South he learned to write in the locked-up language so that a song of his might reveal a secret message to those who could unravel it. He learned to make up the summer-long songs of the Northern Islands that lasted night after night until the days started to grow shorter again and the howling winds began to drown out the music of the loudest harping. We can trace much of Myndal's journey by the songs he left behind him, which people read or remembered for years afterwards.

After reaching the mouth of the great river down which he had started, Myndal stopped at some of the seaside towns. Carved on a post at the great pier of one of them is a sad song that we know to be his, for he signed his name into it in the manner of the older poets of the South:

> *M*uch have I wandered,
> *Y*onder and back,
> *N*ear the track
> *D*ark swans make
> *A*long river and lake.
> *L*ong have I pondered.

This is called a "head-line" song in the older languages, because the letters at the head or beginning of each line spell out a word. And far away to the east of that place, by the mouth of an even wider, longer river, cut into one of the rocks along the sea wall is another head-line song. It is almost frighteningly short:

48

Going
Onward,
Looking
Ever.

He was thinking more and more about the Gole as he sailed, rowed and drifted on from river to lake to pond to stream, sometimes venturing even into the sea. One of the long-boat captains of the Northern Ocean sent a letter home to his wife, with the words cut into an otter's skin and reddened with the blood of a sea gull. Part of it tells of a strange, tall young man in a round boat who asked if he might tie it up behind the captain's long ship. The letter says that "he would sometimes come aboard our ship at night and sing songs and tell stories to our men, and then he would look up at us and even at the stars swaying overhead. But by day he would stand in his small round craft and look down at the water. What he was thinking of we never knew. He asked once about something he called the Gole, but none of our company knew of what he spoke. For a month he sailed behind us, and then at a town one day he bade us farewell, putting his boat on a cart, and setting off overland, southward. He seemed to be seeking something, with sadness and patience." And here the ship-captain's letter goes on to talk of other matters less interesting to us, as letters will.

By the time Myndal started down the river Shirok, he must have been away from home for nearly three years, what with wandering up and back and around huge circles in his sailing. The great river flows down to the Southern Sea through many lands, and in all of them Myndal lived and sang and thought his lonely thoughts, never asking about his brother any more and even mentioning the Gole less and less. But he never stopped dreaming of it or wondering about it. As he grew more skilled and famous as a singer and story-teller, people in the next towns along the river would await his coming and prepare rich welcomes for him. Often they were surprised to see for the first time the sad figure of Myndal, with his lowered gaze and his lonely look. But they forgot all this when he sang or recited, and their attentions were drawn always to what he was saying or singing.

It was down along the river Shirok that Myndal first heard of the mad poet Lyn, whose skill was said to be greater than Myndal's own. Lyn had been a black-smith, huge and dark and brawny, who hardly ever spoke a word while he worked at his forge in a small village. One winter night, as he was shaping part of an iron gate on his anvil, the bright sparks flying upward into the black air, a cold beam from the full moon smote him a blow on the forehead as the moon emerged from behind a hill. Lyn threw down his hammer with a howl, crying "Sparks disappear in the

50

air, but the moon lives everywhere!" They were the first rhyming words he had ever spoken, and he vowed that he had used his hammer for the last time. Most men thought Lyn maddened by the moon, although he ceased to bellow and shout after about a week.

After that, he rhymed more and more, and made up longer and longer poems. But he remained fierce and dark and strong, and men feared his rage as much as they learned to love his singing. Lyn of Lyngorod became famous the length of the river. One day as Myndal approached the town of Lyngorod he saw a great crowd of people in the square, all gathered about a huge dark man whom he guessed to be Lyn. Myndal tied up his boat in the canal and crossed a narrow bridge into the main square, where Lyn was crying out some short songs in a deep voice. "The moon is truth and the sun is a lie," he sang, "And the sea is the dark side of the sky." He saw Myndal waiting by the end of the bridge.

"What do you think of that, you?" bawled out Lyn.

"As a matter of fact, it's not true," replied Myndal in a clear voice.

There was a roar from the crowd, for nobody had ever challenged Lyn before. Everyone looked around to see who it might be. But Lyn started shouting again, and rolling his eyes and tugging at his black beard. "Of all the poets, who is best?" he called.

Myndal had never thought about this before.

"Myndal, the sad prince of the West," he answered back, and it did not sound like boasting because it wasn't.

"Sad is slight and Mad is mighty," screamed Lyn, and the crowd parted to allow Myndal to draw nearer. "Do you challenge me?" Lyn continued.

"Yes," said Myndal, "and I will answer you with my own name, which is song enough." There was an excited look in his eyes now, and his cheeks burned as he unslung his harp and tuned it, playing a loud flourish as he did so.

"With your name?" cried Lyn. "What is your name worth? My name and my fame come from the moon."

"My name and my fame can contain yours," said Myndal quietly as he reached the middle of the square, "the way a carefully wrought cup contains roaring water."

"Answer me this, then, western singer!" roared Lyn. And he asked him a question about the Tale of the Vengeance of Vyord, which is a story not known in the western lands. But of course he rhymed his question, as the singers used to do when they fought their duels of words:

> "Where was the sword
> That Vyord
> Had stored?"

But Myndal knew all the old songs, and answered back in a flash:

> "On the hill
> Of Tyl
> AND MYL!"

and Myndal accompanied his last line by a rapid running of tones on his harp that only he was known to play. The crowd buzzed noisily at this, for the answer was correct, and moreover, the last line contained the letters of Myndal's own name, redesigned into the answer.

Lyn tried again. This time he tried Myndal with a question about the very ancient song called The Struggle Between Earth and Water:

> "What did clay
> Once say
> To the great bay?"

Myndal again answered in song, and again hid his name in the response:

> "Stand and
> Unhand
> MY LAND"

which was also correct. Lyn got more and more furious, and finally began to sing, without words, a loud, wavering melody, starting very low and gradually getting higher. Then he stopped suddenly, and there was a silence in the square of Lyngorod, during which all of the watchers stared at their feet uncomfortably and only Myndal looked steadily at his opponent. Finally Lyn called out, with a great rolling of eyes and brandishing of hands:

> "Where is the sole,
> Whole
> Gole?"

Myndal stood in silence, as if struck by the same moonbeam that had hit Lyn so long ago. Was this not the question about which he had brooded for so long? If he had learned nothing in all his searching and journeying, what could he say now? But he took up his harp and played on it the same melody that Lyn had sung before he asked the question, but played twice as fast and with many musical ornaments. And when this was over, Myndal found himself singing out an answer, almost without knowing why, an answer that clearly marked him as the winner of this strange songmatch. Myndal sang:

> "Within!
> I win,
> MAD LYN!"

And of course he had won, and he had fulfilled his promise that Lyn's name could be contained in his own. Lyn stood still for a moment, raised his eyes to the sun, howled and shouted and then fell in a daze to the paved stones of the square. When he awoke an hour later, he asked only to be led to a forge so that he might be a blacksmith again. But Myndal was led off in a cheering procession for a week of feasting and celebration, for it was a time of spring holidays in Lyngorod.

The Lyngorod town records tell us that Myndal left at the end of the next week, and that he sailed off down the great river. But he now moved like a man of great determination, sure of where he is going. Perhaps, as the broad wheat fields on the river banks glided by, he thought about what he had meant by his last rhyming answer to Lyn. Perhaps it was then that he began to decide that the Gole, whatever it was, lay hidden somewhere within himself, that his search would never end by his reaching some place, or by finding some thing or by doing some deed. We do know, from the sixth book of the *Song of the River Shirok*, how:

> That was the spring
> When Myndal the singer
> Sped down the waves
> Of the wide river,
> Down toward the sea
> And its bright beaches,
> Reaching its shores

As the nights shortened
And the air hummed
With the heat of summer.

It was a hot summer afternoon, indeed, when
Myndal's round-boat was washed up the end of a
little rivulet, one of the many that fanned out from the
river Shirok like the fingers of a hand reaching for the
wide sea. With his shadow still short behind him,
Myndal abandoned his boat by a clump of rushes and
began to walk over the sand hills toward the shore.
One of the many songs he composed later when he
was very old, and from which we know how this part
of the Story of the Gole ended, tells us that he had no
more doubts about the Gole or what or where it was
as he walked along:

The sun was moving downward at my right hand
As I wandered toward the water over bright sand.
On the left, my shadow lengthened
And within me, I was strengthened
As I felt that, on this shore,
All I had been looking for
Was nearer
And clearer
Than it ever was before.

Late that afternoon, Myndal reached the sea at a
wide bay that swung around a glittering mountain of
rock. The tide was out, and the small, far waves were
sighing on long stretches of damp sand, now turned a
cool brick-red by the lowering sun. At one end of the
beach, not far from the foot of the jagged mountain,
Myndal saw a group of cloaked figures, some sitting
on the sand, some walking about together. As he drew
nearer, Myndal could see that some of them carried
musical instruments, others old books, beautifully
bound, and as he drew nearer still, one of the figures
moved toward him with arms outstretched.

"Welcome, Myndal," said the man coming toward
him, "to the Beach of the Singers. We have been
waiting for you."

Now that Myndal could make out the man's face,
he recognized him. From his short, fair beard and his
great height, Myndal could tell that this was the Bard

Brangon, a great singer from the Western Islands of whom he had heard much. And as others moved toward him, detaching themselves from the small groups of men who stood or lay about the broad beach, Myndal could see that there were many other musicians and storytellers among them whom he had heard tell of. There was the great Count Guillaume and the famous Bertrand the Plotter and the sweet singer Sorgenfrey and many others.

"Come and join us," continued Brangon. "There has always been a place for you here; your fame has arrived before you. Come and rest by the water, and when the sun descends we shall have some night-music."

Myndal was by now so tired that he had hardly any curiosity left, and he sat down on the sand in the cool of the sunset and stared out across the water. The others began to prepare food, and after they had all eaten and rested some more, some began to tune their instruments. The sun had finally vanished, and by the light of the beach-fire there was a great telling of tales and singing of songs. Myndal took up his harp and sang, in his turn, and it was not until very late, when the dog-star rose glittering like an immense jewel over the slope of the mountain, that they all slept. It is not known, nor did Myndal ever say in the stories he wrote in his old age, what the songs were that they sang.

In the morning, the band of singers prepared to leave the beach for their great hall atop the glittering mountain. "You must come, too," said Brangon to Myndal, "and live with us in our castle hung over the cliffs, where there is always song and time seems not to move."

"Perhaps," said Myndal, for he was desirous of going with them, yet filled with a strange sense that something else was about to happen. And it did. Brangon and a singer from the North named Widhaga held out to Myndal a broad tablet of ivory, with some writing on it in gold.

"This is for you to read, and consider, and recite back to us again," they said. "And only afterwards may you come with us up the mountain."

Myndal took the tablet and walked up the beach for a way, puzzling out the old inscription upon it. And then he read it three times. It said:

A False thing is inside the mind.
Young men lose, and never find.
They never learn what the Old forget:
What can be caught in a silver net.
Though they seek a golden pot,
The Gole is wholly what it is not.

When he had finished his three readings of these lines, Myndal walked back to the others. "I am still young," he said, as they gathered about to listen, "but I am as weary of riddles as I am of wandering. I have riddled well in my time, but now I feel that I am past being clever. Puzzles like 'The Gole is wholly what it is not' do not bear muddling about. But I will see what I can do with this." And he stood thinking for a moment, then picked up his harp, played a flourish, and read back to them, while the wind carried the last sounds of his harping out to sea:

"What can be caught? What the Old forget,
Young men lose in a silver net.
Though they seek inside the mind
They never learn and never find.
A false thing is what it is not.
The Gole is wholly a golden pot."

"What now, singers?" cried Myndal. "I have re-woven your song from its own parts."

"You have, indeed," said old Widhaga from the North. "But have you woven it into a truth? Do you believe what you have sung? One who believed the Gole to be a cup or a pot or a treasure would have no trouble finding *something* that would satisfy him." He was speaking, of course, of Strengal who had done just this. But Myndal did not know, nor was he ever to know, of his brother's fate. He listened, and at length took up his harp again.

"You are right, old man. I have not sung the truth. But here is another weaving of it which I know now is true." And he said:

> "The Gole is wholly inside the mind.
> Though they seek and never find,
> Young men lose what the old forget.
> A false thing is in a silver net.
> What can be caught? A golden pot.
> They never learn what it is not."

There was a great murmuring among all the singers. "Yes," said Myndal, "I know that the Gole is being true to myself, that it is the knowledge of who I am and what I must do. I am a singer and a teller of tales, and I must move among men as I always have. I cannot stay among your blessed company, but must go away. I have found the Gole, and need never look for anything again. I shall move onward, to the east, around your mountain, for that is where the road lies and that is where I have been fated to go." And without another word, Myndal picked up his harp and started away.

"Prince Myndal!" shouted Brangon, as a small dark cloud moved in front of the sun, plunging the beach into gray shadow. "Prince Myndal! Come with us!"

But the tall young man, carrying his harp, stopped only for a moment to wave sadly at the others. "Of Myndal I know nothing," he called back to them, "and of princes and kingdoms I care even less. Welhet shall now be my name, and I trust I shall live long and sing well." And he walked, slowly but firmly, down the beach and around the foot of the mountain.

The others watched him until he was the barest speck against the shining rocks. Most of them knew that the greatest singer of them all had just left them. But only a few knew something even more sad: that Myndal, or Welhet as he was ever after called, had somehow failed the test they had put to him. For, in a way that they could not understand, the ivory tablet, which now lay gleaming on the bright sand, had told in its puzzling fashion a great truth, without need of rewriting.

And as the speck they were watching disappeared around the mountain, far away to the southwest, a new city, ruled by a young king who had once been Strengal, was beginning to prosper.

And even further away to the North, the rain and

64

the hail and stormy waves of the sea beat about the slanting walls of the castle Hrimhaegl.

PART III

Here is the story of Moad, starting with what we have left of the old northern poet's telling of it:

For months Moad and his mother awaited
Myndal's return, just as months had passed
Before Myndal had fared forth
On his vast voyaging up the valley
Against the rush of the eastern river—
Months of much remembering,
Times indeed of terrible cold,
Unhappy harvests near Hrimhaegl
And loneliness in the long halls
And the cold castle's corridors.

One morning Moad and his mother sat
In a high room in Hrimhaegl
At a table together, turning over
The bright leaves of a book of tales.

They glowed with gold and gaudy pictures
Of high deeds of heroes, done
In peculiar places and past times.
The rain roared on the roofs outside
And the fire flickered feebly in the grate
As Moad clapped the massive volume
Shut, and began to shake his head.

"What is it happens to wanderers, then?"
Moad murmured at length to his mother;
"Strengal and Myndal struck out
So long ago they are lost surely.
Both of them are bolder and wiser
Than I, and if they're unable to lift
The curse on our kingdom that came to us
Through something Father somehow failed
To do, or did, or whatever, I daren't
Consider, even, a quest of my own.
In the old books, I would be
The one to win some wonderful treasure
When my bad brothers had both failed."

"But stories are stories, and Strengal and Myndal
Were never the kind of nasty pair
About which you read in books," his mother
Said as she stood and stared at the fire.

"I know," said Moad, "I nearly went
Seeking them out myself, when once

A gray bird with a golden beak
Waited awhile by my window; and again,
When a flying fish, flaked with silver
Broke the back of the buffeting sea
One stormy night, starless and dark.
But the signs I saw were for someone else."

As Moad was talking, a merlin hawk
Hanging high in the heavens moved
Eastward, unnoticed, above the castle,
And right away the rain lessened
And the wind unwound its wildness and lay
Softly outside, as if in sleep.
Moad's mother motioned toward the window:
"This roaring rain is relenting," she said
"And I know that now—" but a noise of knocking
Rang through the room, erupting in echoes
Among the beams of the massive ceiling.
The sound of voices surged upward
And the great door ground open
As Moad and his mother moved to the stairs
And looked below to the long hall.

Through the throneroom threaded a beam
Of gray daylight glaring down
On a figure enfolded in a fur cloak.
"Who has come to Hrimhaegl then?"
The Queen queried, quickly and loudly.

Her voice had vanished in the vast hall
Before the figure unfurled its hood;
Then standing there in the stark light,
A girl in a gay gown, all gauded
With bright, golden beads looked up
Suddenly at them, but said nothing.

Moad and his mother moved slowly
Down the steps of the dim staircase
Staring straight at the strange girl.
"What is your name? Why and wherefrom
Have you come to our cold castle?" the Queen
Asked gently, but just as loudly
As before, of the fair face all framed
In pale golden plaits of hair,
Looking like crowded, laughing cornfields.

"Sothia. My name is Sothia," she said.
"From the Eastern Islands I have traveled
Far and long. My father, the Lord
Of all the Eastern Islands, died
Many months ago, and murderous
Sea-people have since sailed
Upon us and plundered our palace. My old
Nurse enabled me, one night,
To escape from the castle where we were confined
By pushing the guard that the sea-people put there
Into the empty moat, while the others,
Drinking and roaring down in the hall,
Heard nothing. My nurse never got
To follow me over the fields that night
Or manage to meet me in the morning
At a farmer's house. I fled next day,
Wandering westward as I went,
Hoping to find a hall that my nurse

Said would be safe. I have searched in vain
For a throneroom wherein three princes
Would govern, together, a gray country
That my nurse never named the night I left."

She stopped for a moment and stared sadly
Around the room, till she reached the place
Where Moad and his mother had remained standing
While she told her tale. In a tired voice
She added, "Again I have arrived
At the wrong place," and right away
Her hands clutched the hood of her cloak
As if she meant to move off
Then and there, although she seemed
Terribly tired; but, taking a step,
She fell softly to the floor of the hall
And lay in the gray light from outside,
Slumped in a quiet sleep. The Queen
Moved toward her then, taking her up
And, assisted by Moad and some servants, removed
Her motionless form to a freshly made
Bed, in a warm, bright room
At the top of the tallest tower in Hrimhaegl.

All that day, and all the dark
Night, and half the next day as well,
Sothia slept soundly. Outside,
The roaring wind rose again
And wild sea-waves washed up

And slapped against the sloping walls
Of the western part of the wet castle.
All activity inside was kept
Slow and silent, so as not
To disturb the girl's untroubled sleep—
She had walked and wandered wide and far,
As her gown made clear, for gouts of mud
Clung to its hem, and were clotted among
The bright beads that barely glittered
Along the torn length of its skirt.
She had wandered—for her shoes were worn
And scuffed down to their skin-like soles.
Weariness showed on her wan face.

When she awoke, the wind again
Died down, and the next day,
Early in the warmer afternoon,
The pale sunlight poked through
The window-lights in the wall of her room.
Watching her as she awakened, Moad
Perceived that her pallor had been replaced
By a fresh glow in her face. She glanced
Toward him in turn, tracing his form
With her early-opened eyes against
A terribly old tapestry, hung
Behind his head, high on the wall.
Woven upon it, but worn so thin
That eyeing it was almost exhausting,

She could barely see emblazoned a scene
Taken from one of the wise old tales:
A lady, leading by a long thread,
Gleaming and golden, a gallant prince
Assisting thereby his escape from a maze.
As Sothia awoke, she saw all this,
As a strand of her hair hung straight
Down across her coverlet, dropping,
Fine and golden, down to the floor.

Then she smiled, and said finally:
"Perhaps indeed I have happened upon
The place I sought, with pain and sorrow,
For so long. But yourself and your mother—
Are you all who rule here? Are any others
Lords of the land?" She looked at Moad,
Expecting an answer; he only smiled
In silence, and Sothia answered herself:
"No. I can see that none besides
You remains with your mother here,
But somehow I feel safe in this place."

"Here you are miles from harm," said Moad
"And months from home. My mother and I
Reign alone here, really, but long
Months ago, Myndal and Strengal,
My brave brothers, brought wisdom
To the throneroom, and three of us were
Princes together. But two have departed."

"Strengal!" cried Sothia, striking her forehead
And sitting upright, suddenly, "Myndal!
I know these names. My nurse told me
Some kind of story, something about them.
I wonder what it was . . . I forget now."

"Maybe," said Moad, "you'll remember it later.
But come walk with me; the castle lies
Still in the sight of the sunlight, but soon
The eye of the day will overlook us
And a deep darkness will deluge Hrimhaegl."
So together they toured the tall towers
And long, dim, low passageways
Under the uppermost overhanging
Rooftops of Hrimhaegl, while the reddening
Sun descended under the sea.
They talked at times of the trials and troubles
Of Sothia's escape from the scavenging tribe
Of sea-fighters who slew her father;
They talked at times of the trust that Moad
Bore in his brothers, how he believed
That their searches would be successful, finally.
And so they strolled inside the palace,
Till the slanting walls outside seemed
Stained with a cold and stony darkness
When the sun had sunk in the sea to the west.

Many a walk did Moad and Sothia
Take among the towers and halls

Of the misty castle in the months that followed,
Talking together and telling tales—
Strange stories of strife and trouble,
Wild with woes far worse than theirs—
Musing much on mysteries told of
In old books, always abiding
In high Hrimhaegl, hoping ever

——And here the last big portion of the old northern
poet's story breaks off. Only a few half-burned frag-
ments are left to give us any idea of what eventually
happened to Moad; most of these scraps tell us no more
than this:

For many months thereafter, Moad
.   .   .   .   together,
.   .   .   . no sun shone
.   .   .   . Hrimhaegl still
.   .   .   . Sothia with him
.   .   .   .   . seemed like a sister

But if we put all these bits together, their broken hints and whispers all seem to suggest that Sothia had permanently come to live at Hrimhaegl. We may imagine rather easily how much she and Moad confided in one another and how close they became. Moad's mother may have been growing more frail as her years increased, leaving more and more of the ruling of the kingdom to her son. Or perhaps it was just that Moad had by now completely given up all hope of finding his brothers again. Whatever the cause, though, Moad and the strange, sad girl who had come to Hrimhaegl as if to end a spell of bad weather became inseparable.

The last remaining words of the northern poet tell us nothing of how long after Sothia's arrival it was that the old Queen, Moad's mother, fell ill of a wasting disease. She grew more and more frail and tired, and took to her bed, where she lay silent and sad like a long slow twilight. The court records of Hrimhaegl only tell us that the old Queen finally died three years before the Terrible Conquering took place. It was during those three years, too, that Moad and Sothia were married and ruled in Hrimhaegl as regent and his lady. Not as King and Queen, of course, for Moad was ever mindful of the unresolved problem of his inheritance. Neither Strengal nor Myndal nor he himself could ever succeed their father as King until the old man's dying command to remove the curse had been fulfilled. In the year after his mother's death, Moad must have brooded hard and long over the fate of his brothers.

And yet, all that time, there was a land to be ruled, judgments to be made, people to be protected. And all the time, too, there was Sothia to walk by his side along the sea walls of the castle at sundown, at the time of day when what each of them remembered of older, happier times was a solace to the other.

Moad was a mild and generous ruler. Even in the brief three years after his mother's death, tales of his fabulous kindness began to be told throughout the North. He seemed actually to feel what other people were feeling, and even when he dispensed justice it was with love and sympathy. Thus we read in a collection of old stories called *The Book of the Gentle Judges* of the way in which he would act: "And they tell in the old days of how Prince Mod and his Lady sat in their Hall when two river-dwellers came in and asked for justice. 'Where is there injustice, then?' asked the Prince. 'In us and between us, my Lord,' said the first man. 'We were fishing on the river when our nets became entangled somewhere midway between our boats. I had a huge catch of sturgeon in my net while my neighbor had only my net in his. When we finally landed both nets and the fish, he demanded half my catch.' 'Is this true, then?' asked the Prince, turning to the other. 'Not really,' said he, 'for the fish were in my net as surely as they were in his; surely without my net they would never have been landed. I deserve half of them.' 'Never!' shouted the other. Then and there would they have come to blows, but such a strange, unhappy look came over the face of Prince Mod then that they both stopped and gazed at him in wonder. 'Are you ill, my Lord?' asked one of them. 'Yes and no,' said the Prince. 'I have taken your differing views to my heart and there, within me, they will be constantly warring. Whatever judgment I give, one or the other of you will remain unsatisfied. Shall I say *First in shall win* and he whose net first contained the catch shall keep all? It is an old rule. Shall I say *Shares haul, shares all* and the fish must be divided? It is an old rule. I shall be in pain while you are in disagreement.' And behold! the two fishermen were ashamed at the truth they now knew, namely, that they wanted not justice but the happiness that no just decision could ever give them. And they begged the Prince's leave to go and ever thereafter they shared in work and in reward."

Perhaps all of Moad's decisions were not of this nature, but he seemed always to be feeling the pain of his people's discontent, as well as the joy of their happiness. From the old court records we know that the wedding of Moad and Sothia was accompanied with great festivities all over the Northern Kingdom, but they were not merely of the kind that any ruler can command by giving orders. Rather did they reflect what the Court Historian called "the very gladness of the villages and the dancing of hearts on the farms." Certainly it was a happy time for Moad and for his people. He must have wondered about his brothers, of course, and about the outcome of their quest as he had done in the past. But there was the business of living and ruling and loving to be done; certainly he never strove to be crowned King in their absence.

The shining days, though, like the very light of day itself, came to an end. The Terrible Conquering of the Northern Kingdom was one of the worst events in the whole history of the old times, and it is hard to find a sufficiently ancient story-song or chronicle that does not mention it. Of the first, sudden attack upon the outer villages to the east of Hrimhaegl the *Blue Book of Battles* tells us, and of the sea-marauders who left their ships far to the east and then proceeded over the land, burning villages and laying waste to farms as they marched westward. Always would they attack at night:

> Hark! they came out of the dark,
> Eastern warriors, eager for feasting
> Of battle and blood, for armor-rattle,
> Bringing the fire-roar and the sword-singing!

Their approach was so rapid that the outposts had little time to send warning, and after two days of furious fighting Hrimhaegl itself fell under attack.

79

It must have been a terrible time. The invaders were strange sea-people; they fought not as others did in those days, with rage and dignity at once, but with an almost weary sadness. Even the *Blue Book of Battles*, talking of them, as it does of all attackers, as being "eager for feasting of battle," tells us that they were possessed of some cold, sad weariness:

> Pale they were, as if a tale,
> Icy and sorrowful, lay in their eyes,
> Songs of loss and unrighted wrongs . . .

Swiftly and fiercely they surrounded the dark castle, plunging across the damp land, being slowed by neither defenders nor bad weather. They set fire to the outer defenses, breached the eastern walls, and took the castle itself. The Court Historian was barely able to record the last hours of resistance, apparently, before being either killed or captured. The final page of his chronicle is incomplete, only recording how "they came then into the main hall by the lower gate and killed many of our soldiers. And 'Let us fly for safety!' cried the Princess then; but 'No,' said the Prince, 'we shall remain, for our leaving Hrimhaegl now would be like to a soul leaving a body.' And they awaited the enemy who broke into the throne room and thereupon did seize Prince Moad and Princess Sothia and bind them up and carry them off. And the Court Historian himself did write of these things in his small chamber atop the high tower, the while he heard on the winding steps of the tower the tread of many soldiers with pale, sad faces, and the clatter of shields and sword scabbards against the winding walls. And they broke in upon him then and . . ."

The pale invaders seem to have taken no prisoners but Moad and Sothia. They left half of their forces to occupy Hrimhaegl and to rule the immediately surrounding regions. The rest of the Northern Kingdom fell into a period of ungoverned peace, for the occupying invaders cared little for the outlying farms and fishing villages, but seemingly only for the possession of Hrimhaegl itself. During this period we know that the official village records that Moad and his father before him had always ordered to be kept were abandoned. It was only after they were being written again that any glimpse of the reign of the pale marauders first shows up in the histories of the North.

But for the fate of Moad and Sothia after their capture, we must depend upon what Sothia herself remembered and wrote down later on at the court of the Weary Queen, where they both stayed for many months. Sothia's journal never actually gives us a connected story of their captivity and their escape. Rather does it contain a record of her daily life in the Weary Queen's palace and of her innermost thoughts and feelings. Much that she remembered is, of course, to be found there. But drawing the story from among her daily impressions is a little like trying to read a tale of losses in the rustling of dead leaves, or a story of things achieved in the sound of cloth blowing in the wind.

For example, Sothia would write such things as "Today did my Prince go hunting the stag with all the
merry company in the great woods. How unlike their
chase will be to the trapping of rabbits and the running
after the boar we did in the woods of the pale ones!
How hungry and cold we were! How we lay, hidden
by the trees, while the guards searched for us! Today
I look southward over sunny fields; all is ablaze with
light and nothing can stay hidden here, nor joy within
me, nor the sorrow in my heart for the terrible days
that were. We wander. We wander."

Sothia's writings were kept and later made into the
famous *Book of the Lost Queen* which was handed down
from generation to generation in the Northern Kingdom. From its hints and suggestions and, finally, from
the story that Moad himself later caused to be written
into the court chronicle of Hrimhaegl, the rest of the
story of the Gole emerges. Everything that follows
comes either from these two very different accounts,
or from the guesses that are always needed, like mortar
between bricks, to hold stories together.

Well, then. It would appear that Moad and Sothia
were carried off to the place where the pallid conquerors had beached their ships and whence they in-
tended to sail for their home islands. The Prince and
his wife were kept securely bound, but otherwise
treated with a kind of rough dignity. Sometimes their
captors would untie them and allow them to partake

of feasting and song, and once or twice they heard the
pale ones sing sad songs about half-forgotten lakes and
about final sunsets over wide ponds. They remained by

the boats for many weeks, for there were repairs to be
made and supplies to be gathered. The conquerors
never once spoke of their intentions, but we imagine

that Moad had already guessed that they were the Pale People of the Lost Ponds, the ones who, his father had said, had put the curse and the forgetfulness upon him so long before.

But in answer to Moad's questionings, they either could or would say nothing, refusing even to admit that their invasion of the Northern Kingdom was a war of vengeance. As the day drew near for their departure, however, the two royal prisoners were left more and more to themselves, and their bonds were tied with less and less care. One night, when the nearby fir forest was alive with the hooting of owls and the full moon lit the way toward it from the beach with a broad swath of silver, the princess awoke to a loud whisper.

"Sothia?"

"Moad? Is it you?"

"I believe I can untie my hands. We will try to escape when the moon goes behind the tops of the fir trees."

"But then where shall we go, my Prince?" asked Sothia.

"Through the forests and then southward," Moad replied. "We must rest and hide and plan before we try to return home."

And so, indeed, they escaped that night, running toward the woods while their guards either dozed or were called away to help load the ships. But going through the forests was no easy matter, for they were

wild and deep and stretched for miles and miles southward from the sea. They had hard going for several
weeks, and lived as though they were lost children in
the dark forest, eating nuts and berries, sometimes
trapping a small beast, sleeping on beds of leaves or
dead fir boughs. After the first night, their pursuers
dropped away, and Moad and Sothia no longer moved
as one does when one goes away from something, but
with the new hope of moving forward toward something else.

When the forest finally thinned out abruptly and
came to an end in plowed fields along a broad river,
both Moad and Sothia were utterly exhausted. Their
appearance was not in the least regal, what with clothes
torn almost to tatters, scratches and scrapes on their
arms, faces and legs, and a general look of forlorn
despair about them. But after spending the night at a
hospitable farmer's hut, they made their way, considerably brighter and fresher, to the nearest town.

The town itself was very strange. After the neat,
prosperous look of the countryside lying all about,
Moad and Sothia were surprised to find an old, walled
city seemingly dying of neglect. Stonework in the
walls of houses and public buildings was crumbling.
Few people were about in the streets, and those to be
found there ambled slowly along without appearing
to notice each other's presence, but they were not
ignoring each other in the way of bustling, over-busy

86

citizens of flourishing towns. The market square was less than half filled, even though this was apparently market day, and what was for sale was meagre and poor.

Moad and Sothia soon learned that the town had once been the capital city of a great kingdom, but that the Queen of that land had long since moved away from it. An old man who sat always in the market with a basket half full of dried mushrooms told them of how the Queen would move from one city in her kingdom to another, living there for a while and leaving the empty shell of a town behind her when she moved on. "She is a-wearied of moving," he said.

"Then why does she not set her court down somewhere?" asked Moad.

"She is a-wearied of staying still, for all that," said the old man.

87

"Why?" enquired Sothia.

"That I cannot say," he replied, "but she surely carries her weariness with her wherever she may go."

"How can we find this Queen of yours?" asked Moad.

"Only follow the used-up towns," the old man said.

And so they did. For weeks they wandered south and westward, from town to town. Sometimes Moad would help in the fields for a day or two to earn them some shelter and a bit of food for the night. On two occasions a kindly peasant gave them a little clothing. But at no time did Moad attempt to tell anyone their story, nor reveal who they really were. Time after time they would come to an idle, run-down city or village, and they would know that the Queen had stayed there and abandoned it. Somehow, none of the inhabitants of these places seemed to have any desire to work or to play, to gain or to spend. Finally, they came to a town that was a little more lively than the others had been. Markets were full; people and animals moved themselves and the bundles they carried through the streets at a slightly better pace; flags and pennons flew from the towers of the old palace.

"Surely," said Moad, "the Queen must be in residence here." And ascertaining that it was on that very afternoon that the Queen would hold audience for the people of the town, Moad and Sothia walked into the courtyard and were admitted to the palace's great old throneroom.

Within was a scene of some activity. Ministers and minor court officials bustled about, talking to the townspeople who waited in turn to have their problems considered. On a huge throne at the end of the room sat an old woman in regal robes but with no crown; nevertheless, her head was bent forward as if it carried a very heavy weight. Her golden crown lay on a red cushion before her. Moad and Sothia approached an official and asked to speak to the Queen. They said only that they were strangers who asked her hospitality and help. After a while, they were led up to the throne itself.

Suddenly, a hush fell over the whole room. The old Queen raised her head slightly and rested it on her chin as she regarded Moad and Sothia before her. Then she waved her hand in a weak, tired way, and all the waiting citizens withdrew, leaving only a few guards and

court officers. Then she spoke, with a quiet voice whose sound neither rose nor fell, but seemed to hang in the air like a cloud. "You are lost, princely people," she announced.

"Yes." Moad said nothing more than that.

"Your land has been overrun."

"That is so."

"You have two lost brothers."

At this, Moad could not contain himself. "How do you know these things?" he asked.

The Queen pointed to her wrinkled brow. "What do you see here that weighs so much?" she enquired in return. Moad said nothing, and she went on: "All of what I know I have been made to remember. I can forget nothing, and so it is as if I knew with different ways of knowing from most people. And yet all I remember is part of one thing only." Here the Queen looked sadly off into the middle of the vast room and, as if Moad and Sothia were not there, slowly sang to herself a song with a tune so plain and slow it seemed impossible to remember:

> "Fires will freeze when water burns,
>   A hundred is just ten times ten,
>   The only road that never turns
>   Runs back into itself again.

Round it goes
As around I sing;
What the whole world knows
Lies inside a ring."

She stopped then, suddenly recalling her visitors'
presence. "An old song," she said sadly, "and one that
becomes more true every time a clock ticks anywhere."

"Is it of knowing all this, then, that you are weary?"
asked Sothia.

"It is almost too heavy a weight to bear," replied the
Queen. "Wouldn't you begin to tire of being aware
of things if everything you saw or read or dreamed or
heard of, everything you learned, all meant the same
thing?" And here the Queen sang a second verse of
her song:

"Too far ahead is right behind,
    Too far north will take you south:
The largest serpent you can find
    Has its own tail in its mouth.

    Round it goes
    As around I sing;
    What the whole world knows
    Lies inside a ring."

"What is it then," asked Moad, "that one thing that everything means?"

"No," said the Weary Queen then, "I have nothing against you and no desire to see you suffer as I do. I won't tell you; it was asking just such a question, and having it answered in truth, that brought me to this pass."

"When was that?" asked Sothia.

"When I was young and first a queen, and ever so anxious to rule well. I wanted to govern my cities with my head rather than with my heart, and so I sought the advice of all the most learned men I could find. Professors of this and Doctors of that moved into my palace, with books and measuring instruments that collected dust in every room. Every day I tried to learn nineteen new and useful things, and I suppose I could have gone on like that for years and years."

"What happened then?" inquired Moad.

"The trouble was," went on the Queen, "that so much knowledge has to be kept somewhere. There's room in one's head, I discovered, for all the facts in the world, but not for the other things that keep all the different facts in separate places. The tree of knowledge has many branches, and all those limbs and twigs take up more room than the fruit. Each day I would learn nineteen things: for example 1. Where the swallows go in the autumn; 2. Why pictures look like things; 3. Whether or not flowers feel; 4. How far away the

Impossible Islands are; 5. Who made the first pudding
and why he called it a 'pudding'; 6. How to make bees
swarm; 7. What question had best not be asked;
8. How to make a harp sound without touching it;
9. Whether an image is *on* a mirror, or *in* it, or *behind*
it; 10. When 'right now' becomes just a minute ago;
11.—"

"Excuse me," said Moad, "but you're wearying me
with your list."

"In any case," the Queen remarked, "try sorting
those out into neat boxes. Every day it grew more difficult to keep things where they belonged, and everything I had learned became involved with everything
else. One day at noon after I had just learned my ninth
thing for the day, the bright sun flashed in my eyes
and it was as if the inside of my head had burst into
flame. And suddenly I realized that everything I knew,
everything there was to know, only meant one thing.
I could go on learning and never forgetting, but all
facts and thoughts and truths were like ripples across
water now, not like grapes being crammed into one's
mouth. There was always room for more. Except . . .
except that it has made me very sad, and very very tired
of being sad."

"But how is it that you know about me, and my
brothers?" Moad asked again.

The Queen sighed. "I have only to consider the One
Truth," she said, "and anything I wish to know is, of

course, but a part of it."

"Then can you tell me why I am here and what I wish to know?" Moad continued.

"Oh, yes," the Queen went on. "And I'll tell you all there is to know about it in due course."

"But when will that be?" asked Sothia with a touch of another kind of weariness in *her* voice.

"When the time comes to leave this place. Meanwhile, rest here in the palace, and be comfortable and contented for a while. Then I will tell you what I can."

And with that the Queen clapped her hands and summoned servants, and they led Moad and Sothia into a bright stone chamber, high in the castle, that overlooked broad fields and meadows, with a large patch of woods behind them. In the distance behind the woods there was a high mountain that looked pale blue in the clear sunlight. It was here that they stayed for several months. Clothed by the Master of the Palace Wardrobe, fed and entertained as befit their royal state, they lived for a while at peace.

But every day at sundown, when the shadows of the towers of the palace stretched out along the fields as seen from their window, Moad would go to the Queen and ask for the help of her knowledge. And every day she would say, "Not yet. The time will come." And every day Moad would walk sadly up the steps to their chamber again. Sometimes he would go and hunt with some of the courtiers, sometimes he would take part in contests and celebrations. But always he thought of his father, his brothers and the conquering of Hrimhaegl, and every day he wept some.

Sothia meanwhile wandered about the castle, kept her journal, and read much in the palace library. She learned of great deeds and battles, and of far-away places, and she even read from time to time of a wonderful, powerful, lost object, called by some storytellers the Goll or Gole. Nobody seemed to know what it really was, and Sothia herself had no cause to guess how important the Gole may have been to Moad's family. But each night she would tell Moad of what she had learned from the old books, and each night Moad would tell her what he had heard in court, or in the town, of all the world's news.

Finally, one cold, gray autumn morning, the Queen called out to her courtiers, "I am weary of all things, but most of all of this place. Let us go to another one."

At once there began a great hurry of preparation for departure, as the whole court prepared to move, at short notice, the way it had done countless times before. Moad and Sothia came to the Queen and reminded her of her promise to tell them what she knew. "Well, then," said the Weary Queen, "When all things are One, then nothing in particular matters very much. Your brothers are both well and happy and very successful, to boot. Don't bother looking for them; one had a strong arm and the other a splendid

head, and each took his own way. Forget them. You must take your way, for it is the only one left."

"What can I do, then, about the Curse and the Pale People?" asked Moad.

"Do? Do?" moaned the Queen. "Do you think that the Great Problems are managed in the easy, old ways? Do you think that by rushing off and killing some strange beast, or by craftily solving some knotty puzzle, you discover the wrongs of the past? Your brothers thought so, and by succeeding in one part of life they failed in another."

"What is my way, then?" asked Moad.

"Obviously, the way of the wise heart," answered the Queen. "The outward part of it all is not difficult. Follow the prophecy. Go toward the mountain. Be borne beyond it. Follow your brothers, and yet do not fall into their track."

"How?" asked Moad again.

"The Gole, the Gole," sighed the Queen. "You must go after the Gole without making their mistakes. The rest is easy. The Pale People have always guarded it, and when he was young, your father conquered them. He came from a Southern Kingdom in quest of the Gole, but after he had found its guardians and subdued them, he refused even to look at the Gole or to try to possess it. It was as if he was afraid that finding the Gole would change him into someone else, and he wanted only to be a mighty king."

"But what is the Gole?" asked Sothia. "I have read much of it and have learned little."

"I know all things and One thing," answered the Weary Queen. "But the Gole is beyond all knowing; it is not at all part of everything else. Yet I know that Moad's father seemed, at the end, to be afraid of it, and turned his back upon it. The Pale People were insulted after having been injured. They cursed him. He forgot who he was, where he had come from, and what he had done. But with all of his strength, pride, and cunning he moved northward, came to Hrimhaegl, married the daughter of the old King, and ruled his country. You know the rest."

"But where must I go?" asked Moad for the last time. The Queen pointed out across the fields toward the pale blue mountain.

"There," she said, "and do not fail. Remember that there are all kinds of failure. Your brothers were neither weak, nor foolish, nor dishonest even to themselves. And yet, at the crucial moment, each of them could only find it in him to do what he was best at. Heroes must be astonishing—remember that. Now go; I am weary even of you." And with that, the Queen sighed long and loud, waved her hand weakly toward her ministers and chancellors, and walked down the length of her throneroom. She never looked back at Moad and Sothia.

No sooner had the Queen and her court departed from the castle, than Moad prepared for his journey to the distant mountain. He bathed and changed into the simple clothes of a court page. Then, taking food for a three days' journey, he went to bid Sothia good-bye. He found her at the palace gate, dressed more or less as he was, and obviously prepared to go along with him.

"There is no reason for me to remain here," she began, as he started to object. "I shall go with you as far as I can." And with that, they set off together.

They crossed the broad fields, first. They were all rough, tan stubble, littered about with ungathered oat straw, giving way, finally, to the outer edge of a dark, deep pinewood. Moving into it from the fields was like crossing a line from day into night, and they stopped for a moment. "Sothia," said Moad after a minute or two, "everything is happening very quickly now. I feel as if what I do now were being decided somewhere else."

"Yes," said Sothia, "you are fulfilling a prophecy. But this is the easy part of it all, I think." Then they pushed on together into the forest, until the last slanting rays of the sun that sliced in through the outer trees had vanished. They lay down on soft bedded pine needles and slept. In the morning they moved on again.

But now, as they moved past the deepest part of the forest out toward sunlight on the other side, they were already moving upward as well. The ground sloped constantly higher and higher, and when they emerged on a grassy mountain meadow the air was considerably colder than it had been before. Even though their uphill course was slower than the trek across the fields and through the wood, to Moad and Sothia it seemed as if they were moving ever more quickly. Ahead of them, the bare rocky peak of the mountain loomed up, and at its very top, a snow-covered summit. Their path grew more and more twisted and steep, and finally they turned a rocky corner only to find a huge boulder blocking their way.

"Moad," said Sothia, "this can never be the right course. You are trying to go *up* the mountain, when it was predicted that you would be borne beyond it."

"But how else to get over it or past it?" Moad asked. As if in answer, the sound of a reedy pipe came whis-

tling out at them from behind the huge rock. They
watched, drawing closer together in the cold mountain
air, as there emerged at the top of the boulder a tall
figure, dressed like a goatherd in leather clothing, but
of a most amazing shade of blue. He carried his instru-
ment in one hand, and in the other held out a branch
with some black berries hanging from it. The sun had

already started to set, leaving most of the path in cold, purple shade; but as Moad and Sothia looked up at the tall piper, and as they saw him smile at them, a strange light played about his face. And it was not the light of the lowering sun that they saw there, nor was it the other kind of light that seems to break out upon faces when love and joy show forth. For the first time since the Terrible Conquering, Moad and Sothia were touched by fear.

Then the tall piper laughed. From behind the boulder, up along the darkening path that wound toward the summit of the mountain, his laughter re-echoed. He broke off a bit of the branch and threw it down at Moad. "Five of these will take one of you there," he said carelessly. "There is no need to go any further along this path." And he laughed once more as he put his pipe to his mouth and began to blow a high, thin tune. Then he vanished behind the boulder again, and there was nothing of him but the sound of his pipe and the clump of berries that lay on the path in front of Moad.

Moad picked them up, and together he and Sothia looked at the strange, black fruit that hung singly, like bells, one from a stem, along the piece of branch. Neither of them said what they both must have been thinking, namely that there were only five berries, all in all. There was a long silence, during which the wind blew up even higher; the two moved up into the lee of the great rock. Finally Sothia said, "You must eat the berries and go. I will wait here."

"It's too long a trip for one to make alone, ' replied Moad. "How can I leave you?"

"I don't know *how* you can. *You* must find that out," said Sothia sadly. "But you must go, now, at once. It is as easy for Moad to stay with Sothia as for Strengal not to be afraid. Or for Myndal to be clever."

"But I shall take you with me," muttered Moad excitedly. He clasped Sothia about the shoulders and reluctantly began to eat the berries.

"Take my love," she said, "and take my voice to remind you of what you must do. Oh Moad, do not fail now !" But her words were by now lost on Moad, who had finished eating the black berries.

For all he could hear now was a thick silence, and all he could look at was the gray face of the rocky boulder. Even as he was intending to bid Sothia a last farewell, and to tell her to go quickly down the path to the highest meadow while there was still some light to see by, his attention became fastened to the rock like a nail to a magnet. For the whole one mass was glowing with a strange light that seemed to come from no direction. At its outermost core, where it hung out over the path, there appeared a narrow crevice, through which, Moad guessed, he might just be able to pass. And the very thought of it impelled him there, and he moved across the path and into the great rock.

Inside, there was some more of that strange light; it filled the narrow corridor down which Moad proceeded, seeming to hang in the air like a kind of fog. He could feel the leather soles of his shoes slapping against the smooth rock floor of the great cave he was entering, but he could hear no sound of them, nor of anything else. The narrow corridor ended at a roughly rounded doorway, and beyond it lay a huge, rocky chamber, with a ceiling that seemed as high overhead as a sky. "Can I still be inside the same rock?" wondered Moad to himself.

And then a strange thing happened. Sothia's voice sounded in his ear, as if she were standing behind him and slightly to one side, with her hands on his shoulders. "*You are not even on the same mountain,*" she said. "*Here there are no hills nor dales nor days nor nights. Here is beyond.*"

Moad turned about quickly, but saw no one. Then he faced forward again. At the other end of the great room there was a large, shining door; as Moad approached it, he could see a massive stone chair nearby. In the chair, dwarfed by its height, sat a frail-looking figure. Whether it was a child or merely a very small person, Moad could not tell, for only its pale face and hands were visible in the strange shadowy light. It looked up at Moad and spoke in a harsh whisper, as if waking up from a long sleep: "Well, what have you come for?" it croaked, and its eyes shone as blue as

104

skies it had never seen.

"The Gole," said Moad. "Let me by."

"No," said the pale person. "There are Things to be seen inside there, but I must protect them from being observed. Every time a bit of the truth is glimpsed in that room, I suffer great pain. So I must guard this doorway."

"And I must get through it," Moad said sharply.

"Do you want me to suffer?" asked the other.

Moad paused. "No," he said, finally. "I wish to hurt nobody. I shall walk through the room and cover my eyes. But you must lead me forward yourself."

"Done and done," croaked the pale one. With great awkwardness the figure lifted itself from the throne-like chair and slid down to the stone floor. The gleaming metal door swung slowly open. Moad held out one hand to the pale creature, who grasped it in a cold, moist grip. Moad's other hand he held before his eyes, as the two moved into the smaller chamber beyond.

Here there were many sounds, as of voices talking and singing, as of forest birds calling and, almost loudest of all, the sound of distant waterfalls. The very air inside this room seemed to be alive. Moad moved on, keeping his eyes covered. Then he stopped, for out of the buzz of sounds and voices he thought he could hear Sothia again: "*Moad, stop and look. See what must be seen.*" He moved his hand away from his eyes.

"Don't do that!" shrieked the pale person. "Even if

your eyes are open in this room, I begin to feel uncomfortable." Again, Moad hesitated. And again, the voice of Sothia urged him on: "*See what must be seen.*"

Moad raised his eyes and looked about him.

The smaller chamber was lined with intricately carved panels and encrusted with blue stones. Set in them were four smaller panels, like tiny window casements, with what appeared to be painted pictures within them. The pale one beside him started to whimper and moan softly. "Oh, please, the first one," it whined. "If you must look, look at the first scene; it will hurt the least, with only a little burning." Moad approached the frame and peered into it; inside was a brilliant sunset, with a tall mountaintop, upon which stood a man in royal robes. At the base of the mountain, in letters of gold, was an inscription: STRENGAL HAS FOUND HIS GOWL, it read. Beside Moad, the pale figure was mewing and whining more than ever. "Please, now, go on through the room," it pleaded, but Moad walked on to the next picture. Here was another mountain scene, but illuminated by moonlight. At the base of the cliffs that dropped into the sea at one side of the mountain, a hooded figure sat, staring out over the flashes of moonlight in the water. Traced in the sand beside him, in letters huge enough for Moad to read, was a message: MYNDAL HAS FOUND HIS GOUL.

Again the pale one whined and muttered. "Please, no more!" it whimpered. "But if you must, look here,

look here, for I shall feel no pain then," and leading Moad to another part of the room, it pushed him up against another picture. It showed a scene at noon. The only mountains were blue and distant, and before Moad's eyes a lush, fertile valley unrolled. Off to one side of the picture was a gleaming city, and on the right, looking toward it with a staff in his hand was a figure clad in ragged clothing. "What do I see here?" asked Moad.

"If I tell you, you must go on," croaked the pale person, still panting as if from exertion.

"Very well," replied Moad. The other waved his hand, and the picture faded out, while letters of glowing light loomed up against a dark background: MOAD HAS REACHED HIS GOAL they said. "Do you see?" panted his companion. "All is well and we can pass on now." Moad started to move, half in a daze, when again Sothia's voice sounded in his ear. "*Oh Moad, Moad,*" she said, "*This picture lies, in showing half the truth! Look at the last one. It will show a whole truth.*"

"But I cannot," said Moad, as if to her who was not there. "It would be cruel to hurt this creature any more. It almost makes me sick to think of his pain."

"*Cruel?*" said Sothia again. "*Oh Moad, Moad! Any fool can be brave. Any wit can be clever. How many good, gentle men can be triumphant? For once, do what must be done!*"

Moad walked over toward the last picture. Now

there was a hush in the stone room, and he could hear nothing but the cries of the pale figure, now louder and more frightened. As Moad drew nearer, the cries broke forth into screams. "Oh, please, please, no! This will hurt me too much!" it howled, and here Moad almost gave up, a wave of sickness and revulsion coming over him. But then he said to himself, "Yes, this is the hard thing to do." And then he leaned over to gaze into the last picture.

The pale creature gave a blood-chilling shriek and flung itself to the floor of the chamber. Suddenly, as if with a crack of thunder, a dense cloud of gray smoke surrounded it and hung there in the middle of the room. Then it rose and cleared away, leaving nothing. But as he turned to look into the last picture once more, Moad could see, out of the corner of his eye, a small, grayish-brownish Thing, not scaly and not furry, but somewhere in between, drag itself slowly along the floor and out the gleaming doorway.

And then Moad saw what was in the last picture. Or rather, in many pictures, for what he saw changed rapidly and included many things. He saw himself, as if in a mirror. He saw Hrimhaegl, cold and grim in the wild weather. He saw Sothia, standing on the mountain path looking at the great boulder. He saw scenes of his own childhood, and he saw his brothers when they were all young. Slowly, as each picture changed and gave way to another, Moad realized that he was looking at all the things that mattered to him most. And after many pictures had unfolded before him, he seemed suddenly to remember why he was there, and without really knowing to whom or what he was addressing himself, he called out: "I am Moad. I must have the Gole."

Then all the pictures vanished, and there was darkness only where Moad looked. From out of the darkness, a sound of many voices all speaking in chorus arose. "Yes, Moad," said the voices. "You have come further than your brothers, further than your father, and further than any man ever will. You have passed all the tests that others have failed. Many great and wise and strong men have got lost, looking for something like a golden bowl, or their own souls, or even for some great goal in life. But you have kept on your way. You have done what was to be done, and found what there was to find."

"But what have I found?" asked Moad. "I *have* nothing. Where is the Gole, that I may at least see it."

"Oh, Moad!" sighed the voices. "Make no mistakes now. Even as it is said, 'Men may take heart,' there is no taking It. Even as it is said, 'Men may keep faith,' there is no keeping It. Even as it is said, 'Men may have hope,' there is no having It. Yet to have found It, as you have, is All. What you see now, for only an instant, you can never remember. But seeing it will change you, and even more, it will change your

world."

Then flashes of light lit up the darkness. Moad watched for an instant that might have been an eternity. What he saw then was the last picture of all, and at first it seemed so ordinary that Moad rubbed his eyes: tall mountains piled up and up towards a very bright blue sky. But as he gazed at them, as he followed the tiny white course of a cataract down the side of a rocky peak, as he felt his longing reach out at the distance of those sunny heights, his heart began to pound faster. Moad felt a strange kind of dizziness, as he realized what it was that was so remarkable about this common picture of the earth striving to meet something impossibly high above it. It was his way of seeing it; Moad knew that he was not looking *out* at this scene, and it would have been nonsense to think of his looking *in* at it. But just as he could, almost shuddering, imagine himself, cold and alone on those far, windy heights, so could he feel himself somehow expanding, so that the whole world of hills he saw was somehow in his own heart. He gave a little cry of astonishment and fear, and his own voice sounded to him like the howling of the winds around a far-off mountaintop. The vision of the mountains was eternal and unchanging, and yet Moad felt himself to be connected with it as he had never been with anything else he had ever looked at. As the roaring and sighing of his own cry of astonishment, and, now, of joy came to him,

Moad saw that he beheld a picture of fulfillment; of the end of all quests that do not merely lead to new ones; of what would always lie beyond wanting and doing and getting; but of what was more clearly and certainly *there* than anything outside of himself that Moad had ever known.

And then the flashing of light stopped. The picture darkened and vanished. Moad felt weak and exhausted. But as he began to fall to the floor of the picture room in a deep faint, he glanced again at the scene before him, and fancied he saw his father's face, smiling at him and, far in the background, the towers of Hrimhaegl with the sun playing about them. Then he was asleep.

When he awoke, he was shivering with cold, lying on the path outside the huge boulder. Sothia knelt beside him, and as he reached up to touch her, they both saw dawn beginning to break over the eastern horizon. But the mountain they were on had moved, and what they saw in the distance, at the end of a long plain, was the town at the foot of the castle at Hrimhaegl. For the power of what Moad had seen had brought them back home and had brought the sun there as well. As Moad and Sothia descended the mountain, the beauty and lushness of the country before them became plain. And as they walked through the fields and spoke to the farmers working there, they learned that the Pale Marauders had sickened in a great plague, and those that survived had sailed away in their ships a month before.

There is no need to try to conjecture what Moad and Sothia said to each other then. Nor is there any way of knowing. The Hrimhaegl Court Records, which began to be kept again only after Moad and Sothia returned to the castle and began to reign as King and Queen, only report that, "On a clear day did the King and Queen arrive from the South-East, after a month of fine weather, and with great feasting and joy did they begin to rule the land." Moad soon had written down as much of his final adventure as he could remember, and Sothia told only of a fearful night alone on the mountaintop. The Court Records preserve all this, as well as all of the details of the beautiful and uneventful reign of King Moad, and of his son, and of *his* son, and so on. The land of the Northern Kingdom began to be known as the Golden Country. And strange stories began to be told about the Gole, stories that could not possibly be true, stories that told of some precious object that brave princes quested after, for example. Finally, it became only a name, only a word in the old stories.

But in the fruitfulness of the land, in the happiness of the people, and in the wisdom and love of Moad and his descendants, some kind of power always seemed to be at work.